RUNNING FROM

THE GESTAPO

2,000 Miles over Land and Sea

Based on private writings about a WWII odyssey

Co-authored by a granddad and his two teenage grandsons

Luc De Brouckere, Niels De Brouckere & Ian De Brouckere

Published by Luc De Brouckere, Niels De Brouckere & Ian De Brouckere.

ISBN: 978-1-4116-1286-0 (Paperback)

Out of respect for the privacy of any relatives, all names are fictitious.

Front cover design by the authors.

First printing edition 2022.

gestapobook@debrouckere.com

This book is dedicated to refugees around the world risking their lives to escape dictatorship in search of a better life for their children.

Acknowledgement

This book would not have been possible without the private writings of family and friends about their World War II experiences. A special thanks to my son (Niels & Ian's dad), Daan for his help with the digital formatting of the book and cover.

Contents

Preface (1)

It was June 2020, four months into the Covid-19 pandemic. My grandsons, Niels (grade 8) and Ian (grade 7), living in Naperville, Illinois, saw their summer activities evaporate: forget about the family vacation trip, no boy-scouts camp, no sail camp, no soccer camp, no hanging out with friends. Although there was no formal lockdown, they found themselves confined to the house. They were spending most of their time playing video games or chatting and texting with friends. I am their grandpa, living in Boston, a thousand miles away and was asking myself how I could make their summer more exciting.

I knew that, somewhere in the basement, I had a few articles that described the heroic experiences of two ordinary Belgian citizens during World War II. The articles covered in great detail, their wanderings in the early months of the war (May through November, 1940) and their heroic contribution to the liberation of the Belgian coast in 1944. I've always felt a close connection to these men as they were from the same small area along the coast where I grew up.

The idea occurred to me to turn these writings into a booklet. When I suggested the project, Niels and Ian could not have reacted more enthusiastic. After all, it sounded pretty straightforward and should easily be finished by the start of the new schoolyear.

This was not to be. First of all, I had to translate the material into English. Then, two weeks into the project, we realized that more research was needed to fully understand the avalanche of events that took place. The early days of the Nazis invading Belgium and the reaction of the people were especially confusing. In addition, we had to be sensitive to the different languages and cultures across Europe. There were holes in the story that needed to be filled. We agreed that the book should not have any Hollywood gimmicks, super heroes, or romance. When all was done, the project had grown from a "quick-and-dirty" project of less than ten pages to a book of over eighty pages.

Every weekend, and this for a year and a half, we held a one-hour zoom meeting to discuss the progress that was made the previous week and decide what to prepare for the next week. My role became that of a coach: to stay focused on the main story, and to suggest areas for improvement. Most importantly, I wanted to make sure that everything that any additional material was compatible with the way of life in Europe of eighty years ago. This was not always evident to teenagers growing up in a wireless digital world.

For me, the weekly zoom sessions were a welcome distraction, something to look forward to during the pandemic. I could not be prouder of what my grandsons achieved and congratulate them on their persistence and cooperation. It took no less than four in-depth iterations before we were happy with the result. In the end, I feel blessed to have had the opportunity of interacting so intensely with them on such a major project, week after week. The experience was priceless! Thank you, boys. You made me very proud of you!

Luc De Brouckere
February, 2022
Lynn, Massachusetts

Preface (2)

COVID-19 - June 2020. All we expected was an extra week of break, but as the weeks went on, we realized that was the understatement of the year. As the world began to understand what was going on, many things had to be shut down, school, activities, restaurants, and all things kids our age would call fun. We were forced to stay in our homes for the unseeable future.

One day, our Opa came up with the idea of writing a book. A book about World War 2. We thought this would be fun and similar to a creative writing prompt on a cool subject. Little did we know that there was a lot more in store for us. We soon realized that it was no easy task to stay consistent with life in Western Europe of eighty years ago. Respecting Europe's different languages and cultures was particularly tough. Most challenging, however, was keeping up with the ever-changing realities of the ongoing war.

Throughout the writing process there were many challenges, but we pushed through. We never really knew how the book would turn out, but we sure are proud!

Niels & Ian De Brouckere
February, 2022
Naperville, Illinois

Fear Was Taking Hold of Europe

Ever since the mid-1930s, Europe was watching, with growing uneasiness, the rise of Hitler and the National Socialist German Workers union, or the Nazis. People across Europe became increasingly nervous when Hitler pushed his ideas beyond the German borders. In 1938, he annexed Austria and in 1939, invaded Czechoslovakia. In response, Great Britain and France decided to counter further aggression by guaranteeing Poland military security. Nevertheless, on September 1st, 1939, German troops invaded Poland. Consequently, Great Britain and France declared war on Germany but were too late to stop the German invasion.

Other countries in Europe took precautionary measures, among them, was Belgium. It's a small country, the size of Maryland, surrounded by the Netherlands, Germany, Luxembourg, France, and across the North Sea is England. It was destined to become the battlefield once again, between Germany and France, the way it had been during World War I. King Leopold III of Belgium, remembering the atrocities during WWI, hoped to stay out of any future war by declaring neutrality. On October 13th, 1937, a Guarantee of Neutrality was signed between Germany and Belgium stating that "Germany will at all times respect Belgian territory". From its side, Belgium promised to refrain from joining France, Britain or any other alliance created against Germany.

People had strong doubts whether Hitler would respect Belgium's neutrality. They tried not to worry too much and went on with life as usual. It's against this background that the heroic journey of two ordinary Belgian citizens, Gustave and Louis began.

A Long-Awaited School Trip

All year long, a teacher by the name Gustave, was promising his class of high school students a weeklong study retreat in the Ardennes. The school was in Knokke, Belgium, a coastal town bordering the Netherlands. Gustave was in his early forties, measuring about 5"11' tall, and weighing about

156lb. He had a goatee, which made his face look longer than it was. Students treated him with deep respect. Whenever he entered the classroom, students stood next to their desks until he signaled they could sit.

The town didn't have a fishing harbor. However, the neighboring village had an active harbor providing income for over a hundred families. The area around Knokke was very peaceful. Dunes protected the low-lying land from being flooded by the North Sea. Cows were grazing in rich pastures lined by pollard willows. There were no wooded areas, let alone forests, and the land was as flat as can be. A local saying proclaimed that visitors could be spotted from far away, leaving people ample time to hide from any unwanted visitors. The region is part of the Dutch speaking northern half of Belgium called Flanders.

The Ardennes, on the contrary, is a mountainous area in the southern part of Belgium. Dense woods cover most of the area. It's landscape somewhat resembles New Hampshire. The area is part of the French speaking or Walloon part of Belgium. The trip promised to be the highlight of the year. Students were excited as many had never seen a mountain or been away from home for an entire week. It didn't bother them that the locals spoke French and didn't understand Dutch. His students had been learning French since second grade!

Gustave did not share quite the same enthusiasm for the trip. He was tormented by the decision whether to go ahead with the excursion. On one hand, he couldn't face the idea of telling the students and their parents that the trip was canceled. That would have been devastating. On the other hand, what if something were to happen while they were in the Ardennes? How would he be able to secure the safety of the students? How would he be able to deal with terrified parents? Lately, nightmares of German tanks bulldozing the school woke him abruptly. Ultimately, he made the decision to go ahead with the trip: Hitler or no Hitler.

May 9th, 1940 was a sunny spring day. The students gathered early in the morning at the bus terminal. Some students were embarrassed that their parents were sticking around to wave. Parents were nervous; students were excited. Finally, the bus left the terminal: they were on their way! After a tiresome day of rushing between trains and busses, they reached Rochefort, a pleasant village in the center of the Ardennes. Students were amazed that, once they entered the Ardennes, houses looked very sturdy as they were built of stone and rock instead of red brick. Upon arrival in Rochefort, a local bus took them to their hotel about a mile away. Named L'Ardennais, the hotel looked more like a lodge than a hotel. It was meant to host groups of young people. On the lawn, in front of the lodge, was a flagpole proudly flying the Belgian flag.

Gustave was relieved that, so far, everything had gone smoothly: no one got lost and everyone had been well behaved. It made him feel proud. The boys were exhausted, and after dinner many fell asleep the moment their head touched the pillow. They were too tired to fight about who should sleep in the bottom or top bunk. Many wondered what tomorrow would bring. A walk through the forest? They were promised that they would explore a cave on this trip. Could that be tomorrow?

In the morning, the students woke up to the heavenly smell of freshly baked bread. They jumped out of bed and rushed downstairs to the dining hall. As fast as they had come down, they were sent back by Gustave who insisted that they first wash up before enjoying breakfast. They were surprised to see him dressed for the outdoors, not wearing a white shirt and tie.

Breakfast was served in a long hall near the kitchen. In the middle was a long wooden table. Two other groups were already seated. There was plenty of food: plates with ham and cheese, bowls with hard boiled eggs. Aides constantly passed around baskets with thick slices of bread. The students eagerly covered the bread with butter and layers of home-made pear and strawberry marmalade. This truly felt like heaven! A couple of students tried to play tricks on the staff, pretending they didn't understand French. Gustave told them to stop, and demanded they show more respect. After breakfast, the students grabbed their lunchboxes and were ready for the adventure to begin. What an adventure it would be!

The group assembled in front of the lodge where Guido, a local guide, was waiting. For the second time, Gustave surprised his students: he was wearing a cowboy hat. Guido warned everyone that it was easy to get lost in the dense forest and that they better stick closely together. He then went on explaining what kind of trees, plants, birds, and wildlife, such as rabbits, deer, and foxes, they might see. There might even be wild boars! The latter scared the students as they knew that wild boars had strong teeth and travelled in small packs. Students kept asking Guido whether he would take them to a cave today. He skillfully dodged their questions.

Around noon, the group stopped in front of a wall of tall bushes blocking the path. Guido asked the students whether anyone noticed something special? They looked around but couldn't find anything unusual. He removed a few branches and there it was: a small hole marking the narrow entrance to a cave! Before entering the cave, Gustave decided they should first have lunch. In their lunchboxes, they each found a ham and cheese sandwich and an apple. The apple tasted sweet and refreshing.

After finishing lunch, they refilled their bottles from a nearby small waterfall. They were now ready to explore the cave. One by one, they maneuvered themselves through the narrow entrance. It was pitch black and they only had two lanterns for the whole group. Guido carried one lantern to lead the group and Gustave had the other lantern in the rear to make sure no one was left behind. Ten minutes later, the group was standing in a large cavern. They stood in awe of the huge stalactites hanging from the ceiling and the stalagmites growing up from the ground. As they continued, the ceiling dropped down and they had to crawl on all fours. This was particularly challenging for Gustave. His hat provided little protection.

Exciting as their first experience in the cave had been, in the end, all were happy to be back above ground. Gustave double checked one more time that everyone was accounted for before Guido carefully arranged the branches back over the opening. Gustave then checked whether everyone was okay. He helped two students who had bumps on their head by holding a handkerchief drenched in cold water from the waterfall against the bumps. He insisted that everyone with scratches clean their wounds with plenty of water. All this time, he used his hat to cover the large bump on his own head so the students couldn't see that he was injured.

Belgium Invaded, Once Again

Seeing that everyone was tired, Guido decided to take a shortcut back to the lodge. The boys were chatting about what they had seen and were wondering what tomorrow might bring. As the group got closer to the village, they were alarmed by people shouting *"Les Allemands! Les Allemands!"* You didn't need to know much French to understand what they were saying. The Germans were coming. Gustave and Guido tried to find out more about what exactly was going on and how close the Nazis were but received no coherent answers. Gustave realized that his worst nightmare had turned into harsh reality: Belgium was being invaded by the Nazis while he was on this trip with his students! The students themselves were scared and had plenty of questions which he couldn't answer. Gustave tried his best to calm them down by telling them to stick together and hurry back to the lodge. Guido parted ways, leaving to take care of his ailing grandmother.

It was past five when the group arrived at the lodge. The lawn was already packed with other students holding their luggage. Some stayed by themselves holding pictures of their parents, brothers, or sisters in their hand. Others were gathered in small groups trying to support each other. Still others were on their knees, praying. Many were sobbing, their hands over their eyes. In short, the lawn was a frenzy of desperate students who didn't know what to do or what to expect.

The lodge only had one phone, which was in use by another teacher desperately trying to get in touch with his headmaster. There were no televisions as those had yet to be invented. The radio, however, was constantly broadcasting messages from the King urging the population not to panic. He stated that the nation was ready to defend itself, and that help from French and British forces were on the way. The Chief General of the Armed Forces declared universal mobilization: every able man between the age of eighteen and thirty-five was to report to the nearest military base. Gustave was older and relieved he didn't have to leave the students on their own. The Minister of Internal Affairs tried to assure the people that there would be no food shortages. In between the messages, the national anthem of Belgium was blasting over the airwaves.

Later that night, the King, provided some details on why the nation was at war with Germany despite the 1937 Guarantee of Neutrality which had been signed three years ago. The King explained that early in the morning, the German army, standing at the border, requested free passage through Belgium to get to France. The King refused the request as this would have been an act of collaboration with the Nazis. Germany, however, couldn't care less about his refusal, and Nazi troops crossed the border prompting the King to declare war. What he purposely neglected to mention was why Germany wanted to go through Belgium rather than invading France directly somewhere on the 300-mile-long border separating Germany from France. The reason was obvious: France had built a strong line of defense along its border with Germany while the Belgian border, under the false protection of the Agreement, was wide open. Furthermore, going through Belgium was a welcome shortcut of hundreds of kilometers. The distance from the German border to Brussels is only 90 miles and then it's another 200 miles to Paris.

Observing the situation at the lodge, Gustave realized he had to act fast. He assembled the students in a corner of the lobby. Amid the constant drone of the radio, he promised to get everyone home as safely and quickly as possible. Although time was of the essence, he explained that it was too late in the day to leave. The risk of getting stuck along the way was too high. Instead, he wanted to make sure they could leave in the morning under the best of circumstances. Maybe the railroad chief could help. In the meantime, he urged the students to start packing so they could leave on a moment's notice.

Gustave wanted to look important for the railroad chief, and changed into his formal attire, complete with a fresh shirt and tie. In his rush, he almost forgot his hat. He asked around to understand what the quickest way would be to get to the train station. The locals showed him a shortcut which still amounted to about a mile. He walked and ran as quickly as he could, arriving at the station in record time. At the station, people were pushing and shoving to get to the front of the line. Children were at risk of being trampled. Never in his life had he witnessed anything like this. He realized that it would take hours before he would be able to talk to the station master.

Outside, a single policeman was desperately trying to bring order to the chaos. Why not try to talk to him? Who knows, he might be able to help. It took Gustave several minutes of maneuvering against the flow of people to get to the policeman. When he was close enough, he spoke to him in fluent French. He explained that he was a teacher staying with his class of twenty-three high school boys at L'Ardennais. Impressed by the way Gustave was dressed and how well he spoke French, the policeman went inside to talk to the station master. When he came back, he told Gustave to follow him: the station master had agreed to give the groups of school children priority boarding. The earliest train in the morning was at 6:48 a.m. When Gustave showed him the group ticket, the attendant suggested he change the group ticket into individual tickets, just in case they got separated. He also changed the date of the return trip so they could leave tomorrow. He urged Gustave to show up with his group at the station at least ten minutes before 6:48 a.m. Relieved, Gustave carefully tucked the tickets into the pocket of his vest and headed back to the lodge.

Darkness had fallen when Gustave assembled the students around the flagpole. He told them to be ready by 5:30 a.m. in order to be at the station by 6:30 a.m. They would have to walk, as the local bus company could not guarantee timely transportation. He insisted that they should stay together and board the same train car. He proceeded by handing each their individual ticket warning them not to lose them. He ended his briefing by warning them to be on guard for thieves. The students were pleased, and their admiration for Gustave grew even more. That night, nobody got much sleep. Many slept fully dressed, some even kept their shoes on. Gustave wasn't sleeping either. He was thinking about all the things that could go wrong tomorrow: students getting separated from the group, missing connections, where would they get food and water?

By 5 a.m., everyone was already waiting nervously in the lobby. It was too early for the kitchen to be open. All that was available was apples, one per person. Slowly, the group started the long walk to the station, lugging their suitcases by hand. They looked at the flagpole one last time. It dawned on them how ironic it was that the colors of the Belgian and German flag were exactly the same. The only difference being, the orientation of the colors: the Belgian flag had vertical colors while the German flag had horizontal colors.

The kids were constantly changing their luggage from one hand to the other. They had to take several breaks. Adrenaline was pumping through their veins. Gustave was happy to see the stronger students helping the weaker. Arriving at the station, they found it was already packed with people. Gustave looked around and saw the same policeman who helped him last night. Maybe he could help him a second time? After a couple of short exchanges and showing him the tickets, the policeman told him to stay put. A few minutes, later he was back with one of the station guards to take them to the platform. Gustave couldn't thank the policeman enough.

At 6:48 a.m. sharp, a train steamed into the station. Seeing armed soldiers hanging from the doors made the reality of war sink deeper into everyone's mind. Gustave told the students to board the third car. Once he was sure that no one was left on the platform, he squeezed himself into the already overcrowded car. People were sitting and standing everywhere, in the aisle, even in the restrooms. Many were standing on their luggage. The smell of sweaty bodies filled the air. Fortunately, the weather was nice, and windows were lowered all the way. Nobody minded that, from time to time, smoke from the coal burning locomotive filled the train car.

Whenever they had to change trains, Gustave was nervous: how could he make sure that everyone was on board? He couldn't. The situation was too chaotic for a systematic headcount. The only thing he could do was the same as before: leaning out of the doorway to check that no one was left on the platform of the station. Shortly after starting the last leg of the trip, the train came to a shrieking halt. Soldiers were running around the train ordering everybody to get off immediately. Tracks had been bombarded and more bombing could be expected. It was too dangerous to continue by train. The boys threw their luggage through the windows, and then, one by one, they jumped off the train. For the second time that day, students were dragging their suitcases, this time along the tracks to a place where a bus would be waiting for them. The railroad sleepers were too far from each other to step from one to the other. In between they had to step down making it so much harder to walk, especially with their suitcases. It took them over an hour to reach the pick-up point. The students were sweating and complained about the soreness in their arms.

Their bus hadn't arrived yet. After a few more hours, they heard one bus, and then another. Gustave directed his students to the second bus. Travelling by bus, however, was much slower than by train. It was after midnight when the exhausted group arrived at the bus terminal in Knokke where anxious parents had been waiting for hours. The boys weren't ashamed to fall into the arms of their parents. The chaos made it impossible for Gustave to have a final headcount. All he could do was to hope for the best. He waited for the last student to leave the bus terminal before heading home to check on his own parents.

They could not have been more excited to see him, and to hear that the students had arrived safely as well. In no time, his mother whipped up his favorite meal: mashed potatoes with spinach and a thick chunk of ham. It took Gustave a while before he realized that his younger brother was not at the table. His dad proudly explained that his brother had followed the mobilization order and was in the army. Gradually, the stress of the last couple of days left his body. He went to bed and thanked God that everything had gone well.

What Now?

The next day, a little before noon, he got a call from the school principal thanking him for how well he handled the return trip. In the same call he mentioned that at least eight students from the boarding school still hadn't been picked up by family. Gustave volunteered to help out and went straight over. He couldn't understand why it took certain parents several days to pick up their kids. When the parents finally showed up, he noticed stress had made deep grooves in their faces. They explained the hurdles they encountered to get to the school, and how thankful they were that Gustave had stayed to watch their kids.

After the last student was gone, Gustave sat down to think about his own future. Being over thirty-five, he was not subject to the mobilization order. In the meantime, the war situation had evolved from bad to worse. The Belgian army had retreated to Antwerp to protect the all-important harbor. They fought a heroic battle in the hope that French and British troops would arrive soon. Four days later, no help from France or England had arrived. The situation became unsustainable. To avoid further bloodshed, the King decided to surrender. Soldiers had to lay down their weapons. Joining the army as a volunteer was no longer an option.

One afternoon, unsure of what to do, Gustave went to a cafe he hadn't been to for years. The moment he opened the door, the locals recognized him and let out a loud hooray. It made him a little uneasy. He took a seat at a small table, ordered a beer, and just listened to their stories. Everyone was upset that the King had surrendered far too early. They kept reminding each other that Belgium never surrendered in the war of 1914 - 1918. It struck Gustave how no one was afraid to express their hate for the Nazis. They were openly debating how to join the Allied Forces in England. They knew the British army maintained a foothold in Dunkirk, from where they could get to England and join as volunteers.

Teaming up

Gustave wanted to go, but he wasn't keen on going alone and felt he needed a partner. Hoping to find the right person, he went back to the same cafe. Standing in front of the bar, was a man blasting the Nazis for having impounded his boat last night, including all his fishing gear. His name was Louis, a fisherman from the neighboring town. He was about the same age as Gustave, 5'10" tall. He had a full beard, and his face was tanned from constantly being at sea. After a while, people began to leave the café. Gustave was in no hurry and wanted to stay a little longer. Louis was still furious, pacing up and down in the bar. Gustave was wondering how he could calm him down and signaled him to join him at the table. It was clear that both men were determined to fight for their country and wanted to enlist as volunteers with the British army. After intense discussions and a few more beers, they agreed to team up and leave as soon as possible. They left and hurried home before curfew.

The two men could not have been more different. Gustave was an intellectual, not accustomed to manual labor. Louis was a pragmatic, strong man with a good heart. Gustave was pleased to have such a hands-on person as a partner. They agreed that traveling by bike would be best. The distance between Knokke and Dunkirk was less than 60 miles. Gustave estimated that by taking small roads, the actual distance would be closer to 75, maybe 80 miles. Even if they biked at only twice the speed of a good walker (3 miles/hour) they would reach Dunkirk in two or three days.

Louis had a decent bike. Gustave did not. First thing in the morning, he went to the local bike shop to buy one. The moment Gustave entered the shop, the owner recognized him and greeted him with great respect. He promised to do whatever he could to help. He took Gustave to his shed and showed him around. It was virtually empty, and the only thing that was left was an old bike. Clearly, Gustave was not the only one looking for a bike. Minutes passed, both men standing in silence. At the end, the owner said that he would do his best to repair the bike. He told Gustave to come back in two hours. He started immediately, dropping whatever else he had been working on. He wiped off all the sand and mud, oiled the moving parts, and, most importantly, mounted a new bicycle chain. When Gustave returned, he was amazed at how much better the bike looked. He congratulated the owner, and hoping for the best, left the store on his "new" bike. As an extra, the owner gave him a repair kit in case he got a flat tire.

In the attic of his parents' house, Gustave found two bags meant to hang on either side of the bike. He filled the bags with clothes, food, and other essentials. He safely kept his money and passport in a wallet that he hung around his neck. He knew he had a map of France somewhere... but couldn't find it. All he could find was a small map that didn't show much detail. Nevertheless, he took it with him knowing that they would only be in France for a few miles. He then went to Louis to show him his bike. Louis was already packed, and as a true man-of-the-sea had stuffed a small compass in his luggage. It was noon, so both men went home to have a bite, and take care of some last details.

Getting to Dunkirk

After saying goodbye to friends and family, Gustave and Louis were ready to hit the road. They were not the only people trying to stay ahead of the rapidly advancing Nazi troops. Others were already enroute to Dunkirk. Roads were swamped with people. Families were pushing wheelbarrows piled high with their most important belongings. It was heartbreaking for them to see mothers pushing baby wagons loaded with stuff while holding their other children by hand. Occasionally, a car would weave its way through the chaos. People were silent. The only noise was that of wheels rattling over the cobble stones.

Hoping to find less crowded roads, Gustave and Louis explored smaller roads. They didn't mind this increased the distance if it let them go faster and save time getting to their destination. After trying a number of side routes, they abandoned their plan. Many other people had the same idea, and soon those roads were also clogged. Discouraged, they went back to the main road, where the madness had gotten worse.

It was late afternoon when they heard planes. The roar grew louder and louder. A small squadron of planes appeared overhead. The insignia on the wings revealed that these were German warplanes. Bombs were falling and machine guns were rattling. People panicked, searching for shelter. Gustave and Louis threw themselves in a ditch. It was their first German air raid. Ten or fifteen minutes later, a different noise filled the air. This time it was a squadron of British fighter planes, coming to fight the Germans. Gustave and Louis quickly learned how to distinguish between the noise of German planes (Messerschmitt) and British planes (Spitfire). A breath-taking aerial fight took place above their heads. In the end, the Germans turned around, retreating. Once all was clear, Gustave and Louis climbed back on the road. A nearby house had been hit by a bomb. They biked over to see how much damage was done. As they came closer, they heard women and children screaming for help. Fortunately, no one was seriously injured. They waited until the ambulance and fire truck arrived before continuing their journey to Dunkirk.

It was close to sunset when Gustave decided to call it a day. Between the clogged roads and falling bombs, they had barely made twenty miles. They searched for a place to spend the night. Not too far in the distance stood a lonely barn. It was already packed with people. They were lucky to find an empty space all the way in the back. Whereas along the road, no one was talking, inside the barn was a cacophony of people discussing the situation. With all the conversations going on at once, it was impossible to make any sense of it all. After a while, the voices calmed down, and Gustave and Louis fell asleep.

The next morning, they woke up early and immediately left, hoping that the roads would be less crowded. Once again, other people had the same idea and biking was difficult. Since leaving Knokke, Gustave was anxious to find out how close the Nazis had come to Dunkirk. Whenever he saw people gathered, he jumped off his bike to listen in. The news was not encouraging, so they needed to hurry. They were starting to make good progress when they saw a young mother crouched down on the side of the road. She was crying, holding a baby in her arm while keeping an eye on her 5-year-old boy who seemed to want to wander off. Gustave and Louis stopped to find out what was wrong. She explained that she was by herself, and that a wheel on her baby carriage had broken off. Louis assessed the damage. Using a stone as hammer, he managed to get the wheel back on. He warned her not to pile too much luggage on top of the carriage. To help her out, he attached a strap to one of her bags so she could carry it on her back. Gustave and Louis waited until she was back on the road before continuing their trek.

Back on the road, they tried to make up for lost time. They crossed into France without much trouble. They were less than an hour from Dunkirk when dark clouds appeared over the horizon. Rain came down in buckets as thunder and lightning filled the sky. It was too late to seek shelter. In no time, they were soaked. Strangely, the rain felt refreshing. Being so close to Dunkirk, they wanted to push ahead. It wasn't going to happen.

The rain had turned the road into mud. Deep puddles covered long stretches of the narrow road. It became impossible to continue riding their bikes. Maybe it was better to save their energy for tomorrow's final stretch? They saw a barn standing in the middle of some fields. As they got closer, they saw that it was totally dilapidated. There were huge holes in the roof, the walls were falling apart, and rotten boards were all around. At first, they were hesitant to go inside. As they mustered their courage and finally went inside, they found a dry spot for the night. They hid their bikes under the hay and were determined to reach their destination tomorrow. Rain or shine.

Overnight, the rain stopped, and most of the puddles dried up. They jumped on their bikes knowing that Dunkirk was within reach. It didn't take long before they saw the silhouette of the city against the horizon. The closer they came to the city, the more persistent the rumors became that the Nazis were in the process of surrounding Dunkirk. French soldiers were everywhere. Air raid sirens filled the air. No space seemed safe. There was nothing they could do except wait for the sirens to stop. Suddenly, an enormous blast shook the ground beneath their feet. A bomb had exploded nearby. Gustave and Louis threw themselves on the ground. It took several minutes before the bombing stopped and they dared to get back up. What they saw was horrific. Little was left of the small village. Houses were flattened to the ground and fires were everywhere. They agreed they were lucky to have survived.

Inside Dunkirk

As they got closer to Dunkirk, fugitives were showing up from everywhere. It became too crowded to bike, so Gustave and Louis got off their bikes and continued by foot. A few hundred yards from the entrance of Dunkirk, everyone had to go through a checkpoint manned by French soldiers. When it was their turn, Gustave responded to all their questions fluently in French. After showing their papers and stating that they wanted to join the British army, they were allowed to pass through. They made it! They were in Dunkirk!

The city resembled a nest of ants. French and British soldiers were running back and forth throughout the city. At the beach, thousands of people witnessed a weird flotilla of Navy vessels, commercial ships, fishing boats, large and small pleasure craft. Amid the tumult, English soldiers were directing who could board what vessel. That's how Gustave and Louis learned that they needed an English visa before buying a boarding pass for a vessel crossing the English Channel.

Visas were available exclusively from the British Consul who had set up his office in a hotel on the esplanade. A long line of people had formed in front of the hotel. Gustave and Louis had no other choice but to join the line. While waiting in line, Gustave made sure to brush up on his English. The Consul was impressed with how well Gustave conversed in English, and without further ado, issued them their visas. The next hurdle was to get boarding passes. They didn't trust hawkers selling tickets at exuberant prices. Making their way through the crowd, they came upon a stall manned by British soldiers. Luck was on their side; they were able to buy the last two tickets for a freighter that was scheduled to leave early tomorrow morning. What a relief!

The weather was nice, so they decided to sleep on the beach. They woke up early and headed straight to the dock. When they got there, their stomachs dropped; the ship had already sailed! There went their dream. Suddenly another ear-deafening explosion shook the earth. It was followed by several more explosions. Looking over the sea, they saw a large vessel engulfed in smoke and fire. In no time, the vessel was enflamed from bow to stern. Dark smoke replaced the blue sky. Lifeboats went up in flames. Desperately, people young and old jumped into the sea to escape the flames. Many drowned as there were not enough life vests for everyone. The ship began to tilt to starboard. For a short time, it laid flat on its side before disappearing under the waves. The disaster became the talk of the town. Gustave and Louis were shocked when they found out that this was the vessel for which they held tickets. They looked at each other and counted their blessings for having missed the boat.

Leaving Dunkirk

The situation on the ground had become untenable. Constantly, Messersmiths were flying over, shooting at whatever was moving: soldiers and non-soldiers alike. More than ever, Gustave and Louis were determined to join the British army. Having missed the last boat, they didn't know how else to reach England. Many others faced the same problem. There was talk that England could be reached from Spain. The problem was that it required a thousand-mile trip through France which was under threat of being runover by the fast-advancing Nazi troops. In Louis' words: Come hell or high water, let's do this. Rumors that the Nazis were on the brink of completely surrounding Dunkirk meant they better hurry. The scariest rumors were of the dreaded police of the Nazis, the Gestapo, who were looking for any and all male fugitives younger than forty-five. This increased the pressure to avoid being captured by the Nazis and possibly being handed over to the Gestapo. They realized they had a long hazardous journey ahead of them.

It would have been good to have a map of France so they could plan their journey. The Nazis, however, had confiscated all roadmaps. All they had was Gustave's small map. Gustave reasoned that the German presence would be more intense along the Atlantic coast than across the interior of France. They should get out of the high-risk coastal area and move inland as quickly as possible. They also debated what would be safer: traveling by day or by night? Traveling in large groups during the day increased the chance of being stopped by the Nazis. They didn't make a firm decision but had a slight preference for travelling at night.

In Dunkirk, Gustave had accidently met a man who knew about a narrow path leading out of the city. It was too small to have any military significance and was left unguarded by the Nazis. They still had their bikes and, not wanting to lose more time, left at once. Along the way, they passed several patrols of nervous French soldiers. They were warned that Nazis were only a few hundred meters away, and that they better seek shelter. Gustave and Louis jumped from their bikes and went to hide in the fields. They waited until dark before continuing on their way. That night they slept in the dunes.

It was in the middle of the night when Louis heard people nearby speaking French. He slowly opened his eyes and, to his horror, saw two people trying to steal their bikes. Without hesitation, he jumped up, knocked over one of the robbers, and snatched back one of the bikes. The other robber tried to bike away but got stuck in the sand. Afraid that he too would get knocked down, he dropped the bike and ran away. Louis let him go, happy that he saved both bikes. Gustave had slept through the whole ordeal. When he woke up, Louis told him what had happened.

Gustave was astonished: would they now have to worry about Nazis and French robbers? From then on, they decided to always hide their bikes. When Gustave and Louis were ready to continue, they saw German soldiers patrolling the area. They could hear them talking and laughing. It was too risky to leave their hiding spot. When there was a changing of the guard, they saw their chance to leave. Without looking back, they biked away as fast as they could.

During their time in Dunkirk, Gustave heard about a safe house a few miles inland from Dunkirk. He had few details about its looks and whereabouts. All he remembered was something about an oil barrel. Whenever they saw a house, Louis took it upon himself to sneak around, looking for an oil barrel. They had already checked out several houses when an upside-down oil barrel caught Louis' attention. It was leaning against the back wall of a small house. This was strange! Gustave joined Louis to take a closer look. Together, they slowly lifted the barrel. To their surprise, they found that the barrel covered a hole with a ladder to go down.

The opening was barely wide enough for a single person to squeeze through. Louis decided to see what was down here. He was halfway down when Gustave was surrounded by three men pointing their rifles at him. It scared the hell out of Gustave and Louis. The men wanted to know what they were doing. They were members of the French resistance. Gustave explained what had happened to them in Dunkirk, and that they were on a journey to England by way of Spain. After the situation had been cleared up, they were allowed to slip inside. Their welcome could not have been more exciting. There was food and wine, and sleeping bunks were stacked against the wall. Gustave and Louis learned how the French were organizing themselves into an underground network of independent resistance groups. The Gestapo had already raided several cells along the Belgian coast. In all likelihood, Gustave and Louis were on the Gestapo's list.

One comrade of the resistance drew a map of France and roughly indicated the territory that was already occupied by Germany. He also marked what he thought would be the safest route to stay out of reach of the Nazis. He did not indicate the locations of any safe houses as this would be disastrous in case the map were to fall into the hands of the enemy.

A Thousand Miles to Spain

Despite their precautions to avoid encounters with the Nazis, disaster struck. As Gustave and Louis were on their way to Bourges, a French city along the Loire in Central

France, two Nazi soldiers emerged from behind a house. In a highly intimidating manner, the soldiers asked for their passports. They wondered what two Belgians were doing in the middle of France. In fluent German, Gustave told the soldiers that they were traveling to a friend's house. The way he spoke German impressed the soldiers so much that they let them go. They even gave them a slice of dark German bread and wished them good luck. Afterwards, Louis asked Gustave where he had learned German. "Very simple" Gustave answered: "Growing up during World War I, I always listened in to what German soldiers were talking about". Next time, they might not be that lucky. From then on, they were even more on guard and proceeded with utmost caution. At all cost, they had to avoid being arrested by the Nazis.

A few days later, they narrowly avoided a deadly run-in with the Nazis. They were near a small village when they heard the sound of heavy gunfire. Was the resistance ambushing the Nazis or was it the other way around? They took no chances and turned around, not stopping, until the noise of the gunfire became faint.

After a few more days, after sundown, they were walking down a dirt road, enjoying the calm of the night. They were thinking about how sad it was that this beautiful part of the country soon might be overrun by the Nazis. Suddenly, the sound of dogs barking, and chains rattling broke the peaceful silence. The situation became more perilous when Louis saw a farmer armed with a rifle come out of the house. The farmer was anxiously running around his property determined to find out why the dogs were barking. Louis has been desperately trying to hold in a sneeze, but to no avail. As soon as Louis sneezed, the farmer began shooting in their direction. He had to reload his gun after every two shots. This gave Louis and Gustave the chance to run away and hide behind whatever they could find. The farmer continued firing in their direction. For their sakes, he wasn't a good shot, and Gustave and Louis remained unharmed. That night, they stashed their bikes under a heap of leaves and broken branches and slept in a nearby brush.

At first light, Gustave pulled out the hand drawn map. They were south of Paris and about a hundred miles from Bourges. All seemed peaceful when suddenly, Louis frantically motioned for Gustave to hide: Nazi soldiers came marching down the road. They threw themselves into a ditch, taking their bikes with them. The drone of the boots increased by the second. Hearing the soldiers sing sent a chill down their spines. Their guns and daggers glistened in the sun. Gustave and Louis held their breath when the soldiers marched past them… yards away. It was hard to believe that no one had seen them.

A few more days went by before they were stopped by two German soldiers. They weren't asked any questions. Instead, they were ordered to hand over their bikes… which the soldiers threw on a pile of other metal like fence, wire, even pots and pans. They triumphally proclaimed that everything was to be recycled into weapons and tomorrow a truck would come to pick up everything. Losing their bikes was a huge set back; how on earth would they ever reach Spain on foot? They were still angry when they saw the two soldiers walking back… one of them was holding Louis' bike by hand. It was clear that the soldiers were trying to make some money on the side. This made Louis determined to retrieve the other bike. After dark, he cautiously walked back to the pile where he saw Gustave's bike laying under a pile of other metal. He wiggled the bike from the pile and went back to the anxiously waiting Gustave. Without wasting a moment, they disappeared into the night. Left with one bike, they used it to carry whatever luggage they had. They took turns walking and biking. They were not sure how much longer Gustave's rusty bike would last. Within a few days, it broke to a point beyond repair. They left it along the road and continued on foot.

A few nights later, Gustave and Louis were walking on a narrow road through the fields when they had the uneasy feeling of being followed. Gustave looked behind and saw a dark figure. They couldn't risk a confrontation and decided to run away. They turned left and right a few times to try to shake him loose. When they no longer saw him, they stopped to catch their breath before continuing on. They walked whenever they felt safe to do so, sometimes during the day and sometimes at night. They slept in the grass, under a tree or deep in the forests… always fearful of running into Nazi soldiers.

Hitching a Train Ride

Gustave and Louis were frustrated with their slow progress. They needed a faster way. Several options went through their mind. They didn't have enough money to buy another set of bikes. What about hitching a ride on a truck, or on a train? In the end, they figured that climbing on a slow-moving train would be best. It would be easy to jump off in case they suddenly had to. The main problem was avoiding heavily guarded trains carrying soldiers, military equipment, and other supplies. Maybe boxcars carrying livestock like cows, pigs, sheep, or chickens were a safer bet? They definitely didn't want to be stuck between cows or chickens. Pigs were too smelly. This left sheep as their best alternative. They figured it would be easier to jump on the train when it had to slow down in a bend.

They sat down on the outside of a bend, waiting patiently for the right opportunity. Whenever they heard a train coming, they checked to see if it was carrying soldiers. They had to let several trains pass by before a train pulling flatbed train cars loaded with heavy construction material showed up in the distance. They looked at each other, and although they hadn't considered this alternative, quickly climbed on. The train steamed on for several hours before slowing down at it approached a major train station. Fearing the station would be infested with Nazis, Gustave and Louis jumped off and rolled down the embarkment. To make sure that no one saw them, they stayed still for several minutes. Gustave had landed on his knee which was starting to swell. To lessen the pain, Louis tied a piece of cloth around it. Except for some other minor bruises and scratches on arms and legs, they were okay.

But, where were they? Once the train left the station, the frantic activity at and around the station died down. They slowly walked over until they could read the name of the station: Bourges. Finding the town on the map, Gustave was delighted; the train saved them forty miles of walking. They didn't want to risk taking another train ride, so they continued on foot. Day after day, convoys of trucks packed with soldiers and military equipment became more frequent, each time forcing Gustave and Louis to hide. They also saw many soldiers driving around on motorcycles with side cars. These moved fast and were harder to avoid. One time, Gustave and Louis were almost caught when, out of the blue, they heard the roar of a motorcycle. It was heading their way. Immediately, they jumped off the road and laid flat in the grass. A soldier was driving the motorcycle while another was seated in the side span and held a rifle in his arms. It scared the hell out of Gustave and Louis when the bike slowed down and stopped some fifty feet away. False alarm: the soldiers got off the bike to relieve themselves. The soldiers seemed to be in a good mood and took their time to stretch their arms and legs. Before leaving, they carefully cleaned their goggles which were covered in sand and mud. Gustave and Louis were happy when they heard the noise of the bike disappear in the distance.

They had yet to see a single French soldier when they heard the sound of heavy gunfire. They found themselves caught on the front lines. This was frightening, as they had no plans for crossing the front line. It was also exciting as they knew that on the other side was the part of France that was not occupied.

Crossing into Free France

German soldiers were everywhere. The air was filled with the sounds of cannons and the rattle of small arms fire. It seemed impossible to cross the line without being detected or being shot at by either German or French soldiers. They scanned the surroundings for any soldiers, looking for a better place to hide. About a hundred yards away was a wooded area. They waited until dark to make a dash for the trees. Staying close together, they ventured deep into the woods. They took so many turns, that soon they lost any sense of direction. Fortunately, Louis had his small compass with him. The needle and letters glowed dimly. They decided to continue southwards. They were not sure where they were: in Nazi occupied France, somewhere on the front line, or in Free France?

It wasn't until dawn when Louis saw a small battalion of French soldiers spread out across the field. To avoid being shot at, Gustave took his shirt, tied it to a stick and frantically waved it at the soldiers. The French, fearing an ambush took their time to rescue them. They were relieved when Gustave greeted them in French. The soldiers escorted Gustave and Louis away from the front line. It soon dawned on them that they had made it into Free France. Finally!

Reaching the Pyrenees

The Pyrenees mountain range defines the border between France and Spain. It spans 270 miles with some peaks over 11,000 ft. Although Gustave and Louis were in Free France, they still had to be on guard. There were daily reports that German soldiers had penetrated deep into French territory. More disturbing, however, were stories of French people collaborating with the Nazis.

They still had four hundred miles to go. Travelling by train looked to be the fastest with the lowest risk. However, they had no money for train tickets. Luckily, it was June, and there was plenty of work available on the farms. All young Frenchmen were in the army, and farmers were desperate to find laborers. For two weeks, Gustave and Louis worked as hard and as much as they could until they were able to save enough money. Traveling by train through the countryside in southern France almost seemed like vacation. They made themselves comfortable and took naps. They passed many small villages, each had a small church with a steeple pointing into in the sky. Gustave knew about France's famous wines. He was amazed by the vastness of the vineyards and the hundreds of rows of vines. Getting off the train they realized that they still had to walk to get to the mountains. Knowing it wasn't far away they set off in good spirits. At night, they slept wherever they found shelter, and in the morning, they bought baguettes and cheeses. They were well fed and rested when they arrived at a small village at the foot of the Pyrenees. They were overly excited to have made it that far. Soon they would be out of reach of the Gestapo, or so they thought.

Gustave hadn't put much thought into where to cross the border into Spain, except to stay away from the coastal areas. Even though it was June, the mountain tops were still covered with snow. They would definitely need a guide to help lead them across. They went back to the village to ask around for a guide. A man said he would get them across if they paid him a huge sum of money, which they didn't have. After some negotiation, they settled on a smaller amount, which had to be paid in advance. The man told them to meet him the next morning at five thirty near a cow shed with a red roof. The cow shed was easy to find. Gustave and Louis decided to spend the night there, so they were sure not to be late.

After a good night's sleep, they woke up at daylight and waited for their guide to show up. One hour passed, then another, and another, but no one showed up. They were angry at themselves for having paid the entire sum in advance. What now? Having spent all their money, they were in no position to hire another guide. They had no other choice but to try on their own.

The mountain pass crossing started with a pleasant hike through green pastures speckled with grazing cows and small wooden sheds. As they went higher, the pastures merged into wooded areas. The shade of the trees was a welcome relief, protecting them from the hot midday sun. Determined to make up for the time lost in the morning, they didn't take any breaks and continued on. The deeper they got into the forest, the narrower the path became. Soon they found themselves climbing over steep rocks with dirt and sweat covered their faces. They were dehydrated and desperate to find water when they heard the sound of a small waterfall. The sound guided them to a tiny stream. They fell on their knees and took in large gulps of water. They couldn't stop. Water had never tasted so good. They splashed water over their faces, arms and legs. Feeling refreshed, they continued their trek to Spain.

It was late afternoon when the forest started to became less dense, and soon they found themselves above the tree line. The path ahead was terrible: steep rocks and huge boulders. Vultures were circling over them. Too tired to push on, they decided to spend the night under a lonely tree on a bed of pine needles. As hot as it had been during the day, the night was bitterly cold. To stay warm, they huddled together as they tried to sleep. The next morning, they ventured above the tree line but couldn't find anything that looked like a path. Frustrated, they cursed the guy who had cheated them. After some searching Louis noticed what looked like a pass through the mountains. Their spirits soared, and after several more hours of climbing, stumbling, and falling, they reached the mountain pass. Nothing was going to stop them now! They continued on with renewed energy, when suddenly, they heard dogs barking. The sound grew louder and louder: it was heading in their direction. They also heard the voices of two people yelling at the dogs. It was too late to run away. A minute later, they were cornered by two ferocious dogs. The dogs were jumping up and down, their jaws wide open, bearing sharp teeth, saliva foaming in their mouths and dripping on the ground. Fortunately, they were leashed to their guards, who were struggling to control them.

The men were from the Spanish Garda Civil. The guards handcuffed Gustave and Louis, took them to a camp and put them in jail. What a disaster! So close and then this happens! Gustave and Louis both didn't know any Spanish, so he couldn't understand anything the guards were saying. They felt helpless and their future seemed bleak. What bothered Gustave the most was why the Spanish had arrested them. Wasn't Spain neutral?

In Jail!

The jail was overcrowded. Up to twenty people were being held in a single cell. They didn't get any food, only lukewarm water. Most prisoners were there for the same reason as Gustave and Louis: They were trying to escape from the Nazis and the Gestapo. They learned that General Franco had changed his mind, and Spain was no longer neutral.

By sheer coincidence, they were locked up in a cell that had another Belgian, Richard who was from Antwerp. He was on the Gestapo's most wanted list because he had a history of sabotage. He feared that any day he could be extradited to Germany and put in front of a firing squad. As the three men got to know each other better, Richard confided in them that a group of inmates were plotting an escape in the next few days. Without any hesitation, Gustave and Louis asked to join the effort. Before agreeing, Richard made sure they knew what could happen if the attempt failed.

The Great Escape

Getting the keys of the cell without causing alarm would be crucial to the success of their escape. Richard knew that, usually, the guard doing the last round of the cells was alone. That night, Richard, together with some other prisoners, tricked the guard into coming to talk to them. Richard took his chance and knocked the man down from behind the bars. He snatched the guards keys, opened his own cell and that of several others. They ran outside towards an opening in the fence made by outside collaborators earlier that night. The opening was barely wide enough for a single person. They were near the opening when suddenly, an alarm went off. All hell broke loose. There was a huge commotion; dogs were barking, officers were yelling orders, and searchlights scanned the grounds. Gustave, Louis, Richard, and a dozen others made it through the hole with guards in pursuit. In full panic mode, everyone ran away in different directions, confusing the guards. Gustave and Louis stayed together and ran down the mountain as fast as they could: sliding, falling, running, and jumping.

Once the sound of the dogs had faded, they stopped to catch their breath. They noticed they had lost Richard. Not knowing where he was, it didn't make sense to wait for him, so they continued on by themselves. It was close to nightfall when Louis spotted a small village in the valley. It looked different from the village they had left a few days ago. They continued their descent to the village. When they got there, the streets were empty. Nobody was outside. Occasionally, they heard a dog barking. They were thirsty, hungry, and exhausted; their bodies were covered with bloody scratches from their frantic escape.

They were extremely discouraged that after two months they still weren't any closer to England. They had two choices: To remain in France and join the French army or tr to find a different way to reach England. At that moment, they chose to go back to Belgium where Gustave knew people in Brussels who might be able to help. The fact that they had no money and no passports would make their journey much more challenging. Even though the prison guards had taken Gustave's map of France, it wasn't a big deal because, by this time, he knew the map by heart. Louis was more upset that they had stolen his compass. They fell asleep in the village on a bench near a statue honoring French resistance fighters who were executed during the Great War of 1914 - 1918 (WWI).

A Friendly Priest and Farmer

Louis and Gustave were still asleep when they felt a gentle tap on their shoulders. It was the village priest, Père Dominic, who wanted to know what they were doing. Gustave told him about their escape the previous night from a Spanish prison high up in the mountains. The priest reflected for a brief moment. Seeing how thirsty and hungry they were, he invited them to the rectory where his sister Marie-Jeanne was his housekeeper. She was a compassionate woman and gave them water and a towel to wipe the dirt from their faces. She made them coffee and prepared a simple breakfast of bread and cheese.

While Gustave and Louis were having their breakfast, Marie-Jeanne took a closer look at their clothes. The rush down the mountain and through the forest had turned them into rags. Without saying a word, she left the kitchen. A few minutes later, she was back with pants and shirts for them to try on. Gustave and Louis were totally taken aback by her kindness. She explained that these were donations from people whose father or son had been killed in the war. Gustave and Louis changed into their new clothes. They couldn't hold in their laughter when Marie-Jeanne suddenly placed a French beret on their heads. They now looked like real Frenchmen! They repeatedly thanked her from the bottom of their hearts.

They were still sitting in the kitchen when Père Dominic came back from mass. He asked them what their plans were. Gustave explained that they were from Belgium and wanted to go back to Brussels. Gustave added that they had no money, and that the Spanish had confiscated their passports. While Gustave was confident that they would be able to find work, he confessed that he had no idea where and how to get new papers. The priest frowned and retreated to a separate room. Gustave heard him whispering to his sister, but couldn't make out what they were saying. When the priest returned, he said that his sister knew about a person who had made false papers in the past. Marie-Jeanne promised to find out more and asked them to come back when they had money. Gustave and Louis thanked Père Dominic and Marie-Jeanne for their great hospitality and help.

They left the rectory and, once again, were on a quest for money. They approached several farmers, but by late afternoon still hadn't struck any luck. They went back to the village when Louis saw a farmer resting over his shovel. He looked old and tired. Maybe this was their chance! A few minutes into the conversation, the farmer said that his two sons had joined the army, and that he was left alone to tend to the animals and the fields. He also made it clear that he couldn't pay much. Desperate for money, Gustave and Louis didn't mind and immediately started working. The farmer's wife was so excited that they were helping her husband that she prepared a hearty soup made with large chunks of ham. That night, exhausted from work, they fell into a deep sleep on a pile of fresh hay. For the next several days, they did odd jobs in and around the fields.

Preparing for the 1,000 Miles Back to Belgium

It took them four weeks of hard labor and long hours to save enough money to pay for the passports. Excited, they went back to the rectory to see Marie-Jeanne. She was delighted to hear that they had the money for the papers. She promised she would contact the person, who she referred to as Ma Tante, and told them to stop by tomorrow for further instructions. Everything had to be done in extreme secrecy.

Two days later, Gustave and Louis met Ma Tante for the first time. They found her house but almost panicked when an old man opened the door and signaled them to come inside. He introduced himself as Ma Tante. Without spilling many words, he asked a few questions and agreed to make passports with fake names, birthdays and addresses. After they paid half of the amount that Marie-Jeanne had told them it would cost, Ma Tante told them to check back in three days. Being stuck in the village for three extra days, they went back to the farm and made some extra money for the long trip to Belgium.

On the agreed upon day and time, Gustave and Louis went back to Ma Tante to pick up their French passports. Without a word, Ma Tante showed them their new papers. They looked very authentic! After paying the remaining balance, Ma Tante handed them the passports and told them to make sure to start memorizing their new names and birthdays. Passports in hand, they went to the farmer and his wife to let them know that they were leaving next morning, and that they could not have made it without their help. The farmer's wife was sad to see them go as they had been such a great help to her husband.

On Their Way

The village had limited bus service. Early in the morning, there was one bus to take people to the city. In the late afternoon, the same bus brought the same people back to the small village. They definitely had to make the early morning bus to the city so they could switch to a connecting bus which would bring them to a train station. Having French passports and money made it easy to travel in the unoccupied part of France. Three days into their journey, they noticed a marked increase in military activity. Often, the train was put on a siderail to let convoys of French troops, tanks, jeeps, trucks, and other military equipment pass by. One day, the train was stopped between two stations to allow French soldiers to climb aboard. They ordered everyone to open their luggage and show their papers. When it was their turn, Gustave showed them their papers while Louis remained silent. They were relieved when the soldiers handed them their papers back. After having checked all passengers, the soldiers were chatting among themselves. Gustave overheard them saying where the Nazis were advancing and where the heaviest fighting was taking place. He now had a better idea about what areas to avoid. In his head, he had already processed the fresh information on how to circumvent the heaviest fighting. He didn't mind that it meant extra miles. Gustave and Louis got off at the next station to continue on foot.

They had been walking for two days when they came upon a roadblock manned by the French. The soldiers denied them from going any further and the duo were told to retreat, quickly! This wasn't exactly what Gustave and Louis had in mind. They had to find a way to get through the front line which separated Free France from Nazi occupied France. After weighing the pros and cons of several options, they decided on a location which was two days away. It offered wooded areas that seemed ideal to hide in.

They waited until dark to crawl from one wooded area to the next. Everything worked fine until, suddenly, they saw a troop of Nazis advance in their direction. It was too late to run. All they could do was hide deeper in the woods and hope for the best. The soldiers continued marching in their direction. Gustave was sure that one of the soldiers would see them. Hearing a German voice blasting orders froze them in their tracks. The soldiers came closer and closer, holding their rifles ready to shoot. It seemed to take an eternity for them to pass. Gustave and Louis remained hidden until long after the last soldier had passed. They couldn't believe their luck that not a single soldier had seen them. Finally, they felt safe enough to slowly come out of hiding.

Sporadic gunfire interrupted the silence of the night. It was clear that they were in the middle of skirmishes between French and German troops. From then on, they hid during the day and, at night, slowly crawled from one wooded area to the next. They couldn't tell whether they had already crossed the line from Free France into occupied France. One thing was certain: the front line was moving constantly. In a single day, they saw French and German soldiers moving back and forth. Any territory gained seemed to be lost the next hour.

It was several days later before they noticed a reduction in military activity. This was probably a sign that they had crossed the front line and that they now were in occupied France. They remained on guard before feeling comfortable enough to come out of hiding and continue their journey as ordinary Frenchmen. They decided that, in case they were stopped by German guards, they would pretend not to understand any German, and shrug their shoulders in response to whatever questions they would be asked.

Brussels, a Safe Haven?

The Belgian border was 180 miles away, through Nazi occupied France. German troops were everywhere. Gustave felt that the best way to sneak into Belgium was through the forests of the Ardennes rather than through the flatlands of Flanders where it would be harder to hide. When they got close to the border, they were pleasantly surprised there was little military activity. Under the cover of night, they crossed the border without being detected. They were less than 100 miles from Brussels.

It was early September, four months since they left Knokke, when entered back into Belgium. A lot had changed after the Nazis invaded Paris on June 14th and occupied large parts of France. The Nazis censored newspapers and radio stations. They had to proclaim the greatness of Hitler and how the Nazis were on the brink of conquering all of Europe. On large posters, the Gestapo offered rewards to anyone who helped to catch members of the Resistance. They warned that anyone engaged in anti-German activities would face harsh punishment, up to and including death. At night, these posters were plastered over by pamphlets from the Resistance calling for action.

Getting Belgian Passports

A few days after crossing the Belgian border, Gustave and Louis made it to the outskirts of Brussels. They were near the Grand Place, marking the center of the city, when they accidently bumped into a German soldier. He was terribly drunk, his breath reeking of beer and schnaps. He started yelling, and Gustave and Louis were afraid that other soldiers would rush to his rescue. They ran away and disappeared in the narrow alleys. Afraid that their description might have been passed on, they removed their shirts and put on clothes they found on the street. They no longer walked side by side but at a distance, as if they didn't belong together.

They were still travelling with their French passports but knew that it would be better to have Belgian passports. They had no idea where to get them. Gustave only knew about one person, named Charles, who lived somewhere in the center of Brussels. He didn't know his address or whether he was still around. All he remembered was the name of his favorite café, "*Au Mort Subite*" (In Sudden Death).

Off they went. Avoiding direct run-ins with soldiers, and after getting lost a few times, they stood in front of the café. Before entering, Gustave peeked through the window to check for any Germans. All seemed clear. The counter was packed with people chatting in Brussels dialect, which neither Gustave nor Louis was fluent in. They stayed low-key and sat down around a small table. This way, they didn't feel any pressure to engage in a conversation. Gustave was hoping that maybe Charles would walk in. Gustave and Louis were ready to leave and try their luck elsewhere, when a tall man walked in. He headed straight for the restrooms in the back. An electric shock bolted through Gustave: that was Charles! Gustave stood up and followed him to an open urinal. To get his attention, Gustave coughed a few times. Charles looked over his shoulder and winked at him. They didn't exchange any words. Charles lingered a bit around the bar, and, on his way out, he signaled to follow him. He made several detours, before he disappeared into an abandoned house. Gustave and

Louis followed him inside. They sat down on some wooden beer crates as Gustave recounted the ordeal they had gone through; after two thousand miles they were back to square one. Charles couldn't help them with their passports but knew about a friend who might.

The next morning, Charles came by to take them to someone who made false passports. It was an old man working from his basement. The place was damp. Mold was growing everywhere. The man took a good look at them and decided that, if they were travelling together, it would be better if they were family. He took another look at them: they didn't look like brothers, so he decided to make them cousins. He promised to have the papers ready in two days.

Getting out of Brussels

During their stay in Brussels, Gustave learned that the Gestapo had intensified their search for members of the Resistance and for fugitives. Several of their comrades had already been arrested. It was no longer safe in Brussels.

Maybe the coast would be a better place to hide where at least they knew the area and the people? Maybe they could try to get to England by crossing the North Sea? Charles insisted that they avoid trains or buses and instead travel by bike. Once they had their new passports, Gustave and Louis left Brussels first thing in the morning.

The distance to the coast was about 80 miles and would take two days. Charles had given them a vague description of a safe house somewhere halfway between Brussels and the coast. With some luck, they found the house. It was a small farm. The farmer's wife was watching them from behind the curtains and told them to enter through the back door where her husband took the bikes and put them in the back of the cowshed. After a meal of boiled potatoes and eggs, they were shown where to sleep. In the morning, they woke up to the smell of bacon. With their stomachs full, they started the final leg to Knokke. It was late afternoon when Gustave and Louis were back in their hometown. Each went straight to see their parents, who almost fainted when they saw their sons standing alive and well in front of them. For over four months they had been without any news of their whereabouts.

What Now?

The situation in Knokke had deteriorated dramatically since they left. Soldiers were roaming the streets. Others, equipped with strong telescopes, constantly scanned the beach and the sea for any suspicious activity. The town was completely sealed off. It was a mystery how they had slipped through the net to get in the day before. More than ever before, Gustave and Louis were determined to flee to England by crossing the North Sea. The problem was that Louis no longer had his boat as it had been confiscated in the early days of the war. No wonder they were depressed: after a dangerous journey of 2,000 miles, they found themselves in an even more dangerous situation.

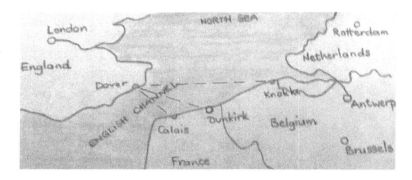

The English Channel
*Over sea, the distance from Dover to Calais is 22 statute miles,
to Dunkirk 45, and to Knokke 85.*

To distract their minds, why not have a beer and meet old friends? They went to the same bar where they had met the first time. They were struck by an eerie silence. There were only a few people. They were talking in low voices, almost whispering. A friend of Louis waved them over to his table. Louis briefly explained what they had gone through since leaving for Dunkirk, four months ago. He mentioned the idea of fleeing to England by boat, but that they had no boat. The man said that he had a friend, a local seascape painter, who had a small boat. He knew that it was stored in the garage of the artist's villa somewhere in the dunes.

Louis was all excited and couldn't wait to check it out but had to wait until the next day. All three went to the villa.

Luckily, the doors to the garage were not locked. Louis opened the door just wide enough to sneak in. The hinges holding the heavy door made a creaking noise. They slipped inside and closed the door behind them. Louis definitely wanted to put grease on those hinges.

In the middle of the garage, hidden below a grey tarp, was a wooden skiff. It was about five yards long. Louis took his time to look it over. He was genuinely pleased with its overall condition. The boat's wide beam contributed to its sea worthiness and the dark brown color would make it difficult to be spotted on the water. Two oars were hanging from the wall. In a corner stood a mast with a sail wrapped around it. The artist must have been an avid sailor. The sail was a patchwork of large and small pieces of cloth. Clearly, he wasn't limiting his artistry to paint on a canvas. Louis continued to check out the rest of the garage. A tarp was hanging over a chair. When he pulled the tarp away, he couldn't believe his eyes: underneath it was a small outboard engine! There was a little gas left in the outboard. On the shelves against the back wall, he found a number of tools, an oil can, and a small container with engine grease. He quickly took some of the grease and applied it to the hinges. He kept looking around but couldn't find any gas containers. The garage doors no longer made noise and, one by one, the men left the villa. Now that they had a boat, they started planning in earnest.

The next morning, as Gustave and Louis were on their way back to the villa, they were slowed down by someone of the local resistance who asked them to follow him at a distance. They were near the church, when seemingly out-of-the-blue an old man urged them to come inside. After some small talk, the man went upstairs. Moments later he came down with two other people: a man and a woman. This took Gustave and Louis by surprise. Who were these people? What were they doing here? It took Gustave a minute to recognize that the man was Richard. The same person who had helped them escape from the Spanish jail! But who was the woman? Richard introduced her as Nicole. She was accused of puncturing the tires of a Nazi motorbike and, like Richard, was facing a firing squad if captured by the Nazis. Both were desperately trying to get out of Nazi territory and really wanted to get to England. Gustave and Louis welcomed the additional fugitives: two extra people would be helpful to man the oars. How lucky! They now had a boat and extra crew.

One important question remained: where could they find some gasoline for the outboard? They knew that the Nazis kept detailed records about who was buying gas, when, and how much. They went back to their café hoping that someone could help. One man suggested collecting small amounts from the motorcycles of members of the resistance. Many of them had a motorcycle as their primary means of transportation. The plan worked! Soon, they had enough to fill two cans each holding two gallons of fuel.

Now that they had gas, Louis was eager to find out how well the outboard would run. He asked Gustave to join him to the villa. Together, they wiped off all the sand and dirt from the engine and put fresh oil on all the moving parts. Louis then went over the mechanics of the engine. He unscrewed the spark plug, cleaned it with sandpaper, and adjusted the gap before putting it back. He replaced the old oil filter with a new one that he found on the shelves. Finally, he changed the oil. Now came the moment of truth. He mounted the motor on the boat and yanked the cord. Nothing. After several more tries, the engine let out a loud rumble and spewed out a cloud of black smoke. He waited a little before pulling again. This time, the engine started immediately. Louis was relieved that the engine worked and quickly turned it back off.

What else did they need? They sat together to discuss what was ahead of them. Louis stated that the shortest distance to England was about 75 nautical miles (one nautical mile is about 1.15 statute miles). He calculated that even when moving as slowly as two knots or two nautical miles per hour, it would only take 40 hours to get to England, less than two days. While this sounded like good news, he told them not to get too excited as major challenges lay ahead of them. Currents of three to four knots could throw them off course. Storm and high winds could overturn their tiny boat. He expected everybody would get seasick at one point or another. He warned them that they should vomit over the side of the boat, and not into the wind. Waves splashing over the side of the boat could easily sink the boat. Everyone would have to scoop water out of the boat. It was the end of

September and nights would be long and cold. Heavy downpours and the constant rocking of the skiff were sure to make everyone feel miserable.

Then it was Gustave's turn. He explained the risks of being detected or run over by a Nazi vessel. They might come under attack by low-flying fighter planes. He stressed that there was nothing they could do about any of the above. They simply would have to take the risk and hope for the best. He downplayed the additional risk of running into one of the many mines floating just below the surface which would easily blow up a small boat.

Louis was still upset that he no longer had his compass which had been stolen by the Spanish guards. He categorically refused to leave without a compass. He started to relax after one of his fellow fishermen gave him compass. The glass had a crack, but the needle was still moving freely. While Louis and Gustave were working on the engine, Richard and Nicole were taking care of other things, like making sure they had enough food and water to last four days. Nicole, who was a nurse, brought plenty of bandages and disinfectants. Everything was arranged without raising suspicion. All they had left to do was to wait for a break in the stormy weather patterns.

Launching the Boat

Alarm! A secretary working for the Nazis in Bruges leaked a message that the Gestapo was planning a major raid on Knokke - very probably tomorrow. Forget about waiting. They had to leave that same night, whatever the weather. One by one, Louis, Gustave, Richard, and Nicole arrived at the villa. They brought their food which consisted of hot soup in metal thermoses and enough bread to last them four days. Richard carried a large container with water and the two containers holding the fuel.

Everyone agreed that Louis was going to oversee the journey. Because a sail would make them more visible, he decided they should row by day and only sail by night. The outboard was to be reserved for emergencies. The bad news was that they would be facing a moderate to strong headwind blowing from the west-southwest. The good news was that high tide was at 11:30 p.m. This not only meant they had a shorter distance to move the boat from the villa into the water, but the outgoing tide would also help them get away from shore faster. The plan was to row as hard as they could before having to start the outboard or raising the sail. When he was asked whether he had brought a chart of the North Sea, he reassured them that he was not worried about not having a sea chart: he knew the location of the many buoys and sand bars by heart.

All this time, Gustave had been thinking about how to get the boat from the villa into the water without leaving any tracks. He was opposed to using the custom-made carriage: the wheels would leave a deep trail in the sand, giving away the location of the villa. Dragging the boat over the sand would also leave a big trail. They had no other choice but to carry the boat by hand. As they were waiting for the clock to reach 11 p.m., they got the boat organized. The mast and sail were put on the bottom of the boat, the oars were placed ready to be used, the outboard was resting on top. When it was time, Richard went outside one last time to check whether everything was clear. He gave the thumbs up and opened the gate all the way, glad that the hinges no longer made noise. All were excited that the waiting was over and that the journey had started.

Nobody complained that the boat, filled with all their gear, was much heavier than they had thought. Totally exhausted, they reached the first ripples of the sea. They pushed the boat further into the surf until it was floating. First Nicole hopped in. Gustave and Richard followed. Before Louis hopped in, he gave it a final push. So far, they hadn't been detected by German soldiers. Gustave and Richard started rowing as hard as they could. Louis, sitting at the helm, made sure they were heading straight into the sea. An hour later, Louis and Nicole took over rowing. Later that night, Louis noticed that the wind had somewhat diminished and had shifted to the southeast. He raised the sail and peace came over them as the sail gently carried them over the waves.

First Night at Sea

So far, everything had gone according to plan. Louis felt that everyone deserved a break and volunteered to take the first watch. The others huddled up against each other to stay warm. Everything was quiet - almost too quiet. Louis kept his eyes fixed on the horizon. Occasionally he looked over his shoulders towards the shore which was barely visible in the dark. Was that a small light? He looked again: it was moving. He figured the light was probably from Nazi soldiers patrolling the beach. A little later, the light disappeared. He let out a sigh of relief. He kept checking the course on his compass. They were still on course, and gradually their distance from shore increased. Everything seemed peaceful, and he was happy to be back on a boat on his beloved North Sea. A chill went through his veins when suddenly search lights swept over the sea. He awoke the others, and in no time, they took down the sail and the mast. They laid flat in the boat, hoping not to be detected. After a while, the light beams were no longer sweeping over the sea, but instead were pointing at the sky. Did this mean that the Nazis were more concerned about attacks from the air than from ships? They had to get away from the searchlights, and fast. But how?

Louis refused to raise the sail as this would increase the risk of being detected. They were too tired to row since they had spent so much energy carrying the boat. Was this a good time to use the outboard? Maybe. He mounted the engine over the stern and lowered the tail in the water. He yanked the cord, but nothing happened. After several more pulls, the propeller made a single turn and stopped. He increased the gas: the engine spewed a dark cloud. Louis kept trying for several more minutes. To everyone's relief, he finally got the engine running. He stayed at the helm for another hour before handing it over to Gustave.

Two hours into his watch, Gustave noticed a weak light in the far distance. It was growing brighter and seemed to be heading straight in their direction. Afraid that the sound of the engine might betray them, he shut off the engine. The light became brighter and brighter as it came closer and closer. Gustave awoke Louis and the others. Would the ship run over them? Would they be taken captive? Either way, is there anything they could do? They kept staring at the light:

it looked like it was still heading straight for them. They had almost given up hope when the ship slightly adjusted its course. It passed within fifty meters. They could hear German soldiers arguing between themselves that they needed to make sure to continuously scan the water.

Since Louis was in charge, he kept an eye on how they were doing. To his dismay, he noticed that despite Richard and Nicole rowing hard, the strong current was pushing them in the wrong direction. They were drifting closer and closer to a buoy. An idea popped in his head: why not connect the boat to the buoy? Why hadn't he thought of that before? Not only would the current no longer be pushing them away, but it would also give everyone a chance to rest. He explained the plan to the crew. Richard stood ready, grabbed the buoy, and wrapped a rope around it. If only the rope would hold! With every wave, the rope chaffed against the metal rim of the buoy. Slowly, the strands were giving way. A few minutes later, a strong wave lifted the boat and the last strand snapped. The current was pushing them farther away from England. Using the outboard in this kind of sea would be useless and waste their precious fuel.

A couple of hours later, Louis noticed the shape of the waves changing. This was an indication the current had turned in their favor. The wind was still blowing against them, so it didn't make sense to raise the sail. All they could do was row and take advantage of the favorable current. With renewed energy, Richard and Gustave volunteered to be the first team, switching with Louis and Nicole every two hours. Louis couldn't stop blaming himself for what happened at the buoy. If only he could find something that wouldn't chafe. He rummaged through the skiff. Deep in the bow, hidden under a pile of rugs was the anchor. That was it! Next time they could hook the anchor onto the buoy which would eliminate the risk of chafing through the rope. This brought him to another idea. They would row or sail only when the current was in their favor. Whenever the wind and current were against them, they would tie up to a buoy.

Second Night at Sea

Rowing was exhausting and painful. The palms of their hands were covered with blisters. When the blisters sprung open, blood would seep out. When seawater touched the open wounds, the salt made the pain unbearable. Nicole did her best to disinfect their hands and wrapped a bandage around them. Only Louis' hands, already covered with calluses, were not bleeding.

Despite being in terrible pain, Richard continued to row whenever it was his turn. He didn't want to give up, and certainly not in the presence of a woman. From time to time, he would change the way he held the oar. Suddenly, he lost his grip and the oar slipped into the water. Richard and Gustave tried to grab it, but the waves carried it away. Louis, overseeing the situation, used the other oar to quickly turn the boat around and scull the boat towards the floating oar. Gustave was ready to grab it but missed. Desperately, he stretched out his arm further and further until he lost his balance and tumbled overboard. Louis and Richard grabbed him by the shoulders and pulled him aboard.

Gustave was shivering over his entire body. It took a while for him to fully assimilate what had happened and how lucky he was that his friends had rescued him. Louis still wanted to retrieve the oar, but it was nowhere to be seen. The waves had pushed it out of sight. They were left with only one oar. Overnight, the wind increased, and whitecaps had formed all around them. Waves were splashing over the sides. A sudden squall almost capsized the boat. They took turns bailing out the water. On a positive note, the odds of them being detected in a foaming sea were much lower. This was welcome news for a crew near desperation.

And a Third Night

It was late afternoon, on the third day, when a fishing boat appeared on the horizon. As it moved closer, they recognized a Belgian flag painted on the side of the boat. Richard got excited. He jumped up and started waving his arms frantically up and down. Louis immediately pulled him down. He knew that every Belgian fishing vessel now had a

Nazi soldier onboard. The vessel came closer but suddenly turned around to haul in their nets. Once again, they were counting on their luck that no one had noticed them. Deep in his heart, Louis was convinced the fishermen had seen them and had come closer to check them out. All the while, the fishermen were probably keeping the German guard busy in the back of the boat. Louis also assumed they would let his family know about their whereabouts. He estimated they were still less than fifteen km from the Belgian coast but at least making some progress towards England.

At night, there was a gentle breeze. Everyone was happy when Louis raised the sail and they no longer had to row. When the wind died completely later that night, Louis took down the sail. Although this wasn't an emergency, Louis decided to run the outboard in search of a buoy to tie up to. They still had plenty of gasoline. After a couple of yanks, the engine started, but was making more noise than before. Louis checked it out but couldn't find anything wrong. After a few hours, they came upon a buoy, and Richard secured the anchor around it. Relieved, everyone let off an exhausted sigh as Louis silenced the motor. Drained and fatigued, they tried to get some sleep. They were too tired to worry about what the next day might bring.

And a Fourth

It was their fourth day at sea. Everyone was wet, cold, and feeling miserable. The waves were constantly moving their boat up and down, side to side. Being stuck on a small boat on the North Sea began to take its toll. Whenever someone wanted to move, the others had to move. Conversations no longer existed. They all seemed to be getting on each other's nerves.

Nicole didn't like that Richard carried a twenty cm dagger in a holster on his belt. She no longer felt safe. Tensions were growing between Richard and Louis. Richard was used to being in charge and had a hard time accepting that this time, Louis was in charge. He even went so far as to openly challenge Louis regarding how he could possibly know when the current changed. Louis' explanation that it was obvious from changes in the shape of the waves just added to Richard's irritation. From then on, the two men stopped looking each other straight in the eyes. It took Gustave's intervention to stop the arguing. Little food was left, and the bread had turned hard as stone. Their drinking water was dangerously low, and drinking sea water would only make matters worse.

Even a Fifth

By day five, the mood on board was well below zero. How much longer would they be able to survive? Would they ever reach England? It was around noon when the sound of a plane broke the silence. Richard recognized the sound. It was that of a single person German Focke-Wulf Fw 190 fighter plane. It circled above them and then disappeared. Richard predicted that it would come back with reinforcements. And indeed, half an hour later, they were under gunfire from five Nazi Messerschmitt Bf 109 fighter planes. Bullets rained down on the small skiff. Everyone took cover. The men covered Nicole with their bodies. Richard yelled: "Don't move! Pretend that we're dead!"

The planes circled one more time over the skiff when a different roar of planes filled the air. It was the sound of Spitfires from the British RAF (Royal Air Force). Instead of continuing to prey on a defenseless skiff, the Nazis found themselves caught in an air battle. Louis was the first to slowly raise his head. Slowly, the others followed. They watched as a fierce air fight broke out right over their heads. One of the Messerschmitts burst into flames and plunged into the sea. Two others were crippled. The remaining two declared defeat and fled in the direction where they came from.

The situation on the skiff was going from bad to worse. Gustave had gotten hit by a bullet in his shoulder and could no longer move his arm. Louis had a bullet skim over the top of his head. Blood was dripping over his eyes. Nicole was relatively unhurt. She just suffered from some bruises she got when she threw herself on the bottom of the boat. Richard was the worst off. He had a bullet wound on his left leg and blood was gushing out of his belly. Nicole knew that if she didn't stop the bleeding, Richard would soon be dead. She ripped his shirt in long pieces and tied it firmly around him. This seemed to slow down the bleeding. Next, she looked at the bullet in his leg. It looked ugly. She grabbed his dagger and disinfected it by pouring ether over it. Without warning him, she dug the dagger into his leg to remove the bullet. Richard screamed. His scream became even harsher when Nicole proceeded to pour ether directly into the open wound. He cursed Nicole up and down but thanked her in the end.

Nicole now turned her attention to Gustave's shoulder wound. The bullet had entered his shoulder on one side and exited on the other. She used all the remaining ether to treat his shoulder, and then improvised a sling to hold up his arm. Then she turned her attention back on Richard. She needed something to immobilize his leg. Looking around the skiff, she found two pieces of wood that could do the job. She tied the pieces around his leg using the last of the bandages. Finally, she switched her attention back to Louis. Since she ran out of ether treating Gustave's shoulder, she improvised and used seawater to flush the wound on Louis' head. The salt made Louis yell from pain.

Feeling a little better, Louis surveyed the damage on the boat. There were bullet holes above and below the waterline. It was difficult to find the precise location of the underwater holes as water was rushing in everywhere. Water in the skiff was already up to the benches. He rolled up his sleeves, and with his hand in the water, found one and then another large hole. He plugged the holes with pieces of cloth. The repair was not perfect, but at least it slowed down the water getting in. Next, he bailed buckets and buckets of water over the side. The constant bending over and the strain on his arms and shoulders added to the pain of his head wound. Once he was comfortable that the boat would stay afloat, he leaned back on the bench and immediately fell into a deep sleep.

Both Gustave and Richard were running high fevers and were begging for water. When Nicole grabbed the container of fresh water, it felt very light: a bullet had blown a hole in it. Barely a cup was left. She let everyone have a sip. Miraculously, the gasoline can was still intact. A bullet in that can could have caused an explosion. Richard remained in severe agony. His fever continued to get worse. Nicole dunked a piece of cloth in the cold sea water and applied it to his forehead. As his forehead warmed the cloth, she repeated the process. She did her best, making sure no water would run into his open wounds. There was nothing else she could do. Richard grew weaker and weaker. It took hours before his temperature showed signs of stabilizing. It was only after Nicole had taken care of everyone else that she took time to check on herself. A deep scar ran from her left ear to her neck. Whatever blood was on her clothes wasn't hers. Without moving Richard's leg, she huddled in between Louis and Gustave, and fell into a deep sleep.

A Rescue in Two Phases

Louis was half-asleep when he heard the sound of an engine. Was he dreaming? Sometimes the noise seemed to come closer but then disappeared again. This went on for several minutes. Eager to find out what caused it, he lifted his body and looked around. He couldn't believe his eyes. A patrol boat of the British Navy was zigzagging the waters around them. Were they searching for them? Adrenaline rushed through his veins. He grabbed the mast, tied the sail around it and held it up, the sail flapping in the wind. The commotion woke up Gustave and Nicole. Both jumped on their feet and helped Louis hold the mast as high as possible. By this time, Richard had also awoken but was too weak to be of any help.

Why weren't the sailors looking in their direction? It was now or never. Louis soaked a piece of cloth in gasoline, lit his last match against a piece of leather, and held it against the cloth. Immediately, it burst into flames. He held the flame high above his head but had to drop it when the flames reached his hands. They were overwhelmed with joy when the boat finally headed in their direction. One by one, the crew hoisted them aboard the patrol boat. The officer in charge was astounded that they had survived the perils of the North Sea on such a small boat. They were rescued just in time: sustained gale force wind was forecast for tomorrow, something the skiff would never have survived.

They were not brought directly to England. Instead, the patrol boat transferred them to a rescue boat of the Royal National Lifeboat Institution (RNLI) that would bring them to Dover. It was warm inside the rescue boat. The crew covered them with warm blankets and provided them with hot tea. Why not coffee? The nurse on board the rescue boat checked out their wounds, and after applying plenty of disinfectants, replaced the old bandages with new ones. She praised Nicole for having put together an emergency splint around Richard's leg.

Upon their arrival in Dover, Richard was immediately carried off on a stretcher and transferred into a waiting ambulance. At the navy hospital, the surgeon examining Richard's leg decided to have it amputated. Richard was too weak to object. Although the surgery had gone well, it was followed by high fever, raising fears that he might have an infection. A doctor also examined Gustave's shoulder. He was confident that no surgery was needed and that it would heal over time. The nurse examining Nicole and Louis was optimistic that spending three or four days at the hospital would allow both to regain most of their original strength.

That night, everyone enjoyed sleeping in a real bed between clean sheets instead of being cramped on a hard bench on the rocking skiff. Nicole appreciated the privacy of a bathroom. Gone were the days and nights of unbearable stress and anxiety. Occasional nightmares continued to follow them for the rest of their lives.

Questions and More Questions

Once they had regained their strength, they were interrogated by members of the British Intelligence who wanted to know their real identities. Only Nicole's papers seemed authentic. Gustave and Louis struggled to explain why their papers were fake. In the end, it was the story about their journey through France and captivity at the Spanish border that convinced the interrogators to believe them. They had to wait a week before Richard was deemed fit enough to be questioned.

When it was his time, Richard also struggled to gain the trust of the intelligence officers. Their attitude changed when he provided them with several details of the resistance in Belgium, that they were not aware of. Once they were convinced that there was no spy between them, they wanted to collect as much information as possible, not only about the military situation along the coast but also about hospitals, food distribution and rationing, atrocities on civilians, the sentiment of the people and much more.

Throughout this period, Gustave had been torturing his brain why the Nazis had been so determined to kill them. Didn't they have anything more important on their mind than to kill a few citizens fleeing in a tiny boat? The answer was staring him straight in his face; at all costs, the Nazis wanted to avoid the British gaining intelligence on their coastal defenses.

Joining the Allied Forces

Now that they were finally in England, a new chapter of their lives began. Gustave and Louis were eager to join the Allied Forces and fight the Nazis. The recruiting officers were impressed with Gustave's intellect and leadership. Clearly, he should be groomed to become an officer. The fact that Gustave spoke English and French in addition to his native Dutch made him ideal for a career with the Canadian Forces where being bilingual was highly valued. Speaking German was a bonus. Within weeks, Gustave was dispatched to a base of the Canadian Army in Quebec. In no time, he rose to the rank of officer and was involved in military operations across the world.

When the recruiters took a closer look at Louis, they were amazed how well he had navigated the tiny skiff through the treacherous waters of the North Sea. Immediately, they recommended him to become a navigator provided he committed to improving his English. Nicole had family in London and wanted to see how they were doing. After staying with them for a week, she returned to Dover. There was a shortage of nurses capable of serving on ships. Without any hesitation, the recruiters arranged for her to join the Red Cross of the Royal Navy. She was also asked to improve her English fluency.

Richard, now with one leg, was unfit for front line duty. Although they initially weren't sure what to recommend, his deep knowledge of the Belgian Resistance and the fact that his brother was head of the cell in Antwerp could be put to good use. He was recommended to serve with the British Intelligence. Furthermore, the fact that he was fluent in Dutch and French made him perfect for the job. Richard's English was just as bad as the others, so he was also required to work on his fluency.

Four years after having set foot on English soil, each had made a career for themselves. Gustave, who fought with the Canadian Army, received several decorations for personal bravery and for the way he led his men into combat. Nicole was promoted to head nurse on destroyers of the British navy. Louis drew tremendous respect from the Navy when he helped navigate large and small ships amid the sandbars and swift currents of the North Sea. Within a year, he was officially promoted to the rank of navigator. He was in such high demand that he barely had time to take breaks between voyages. Richard, working closely with his brother in Antwerp, became the main liaison between the British

Intelligence Organization and the Resistance movement in Belgium. He devised a clever way to funnel money from England to Antwerp which was used to supply the Resistance with rifles and explosives.

Victory Is in Sight!

In the spring of 1944, it became clear that the Nazis were no longer as strong as they had been. Rumors were circulating that the Allies were planning a major offensive. On June 6th, a never-before-seen force of American and British troops stormed the beaches of Normandy. This event marked the turning point in World War II and will be forever be remembered as D-Day. However, another year would pass before the war was completely over.

It took the Allies three months to cover the 200 miles from Normandy to Paris. On August 25th, 1944, American, British, and French forces marched into Paris. Ten days later, on September 4th, 1944, the British Army liberated Brussels and Antwerp. Ever since the port of Rotterdam had been destroyed in 1940, the port of Antwerp was the largest deep-water port left in Western Europe. It was connected to the North Sea via the river Scheldt. On their rush out of Antwerp, the Nazis tried to destroy all quays and cranes of the port, but thanks to the local resistance most of these plans were foiled leaving the port largely intact.

While the American and British armies were heading for Berlin from the west, the Russian Red Army did the same from the east. It became clear that there was more to the invasion than just the liberation of Europe. It had become a race between the Allies and Russia to be the first to arrive in Berlin and capture Hitler. As a result, the Allies disregarded everything that was not directly in their path. For example, although the port of Antwerp had been liberated, it was impossible to reach Antwerp from the sea because the banks of the Scheldt were still in the hands of the Nazis. This effectively cut off the supply of military equipment that was so desperately needed for the rapidly advancing Allies. The Nazis were determined to keep it that way and turned the area around the river into a formidable fortress with extra troops and equipment.

By September 8th, 1944, all cities along the Belgian coast had been liberated except for a small area around Knokke near the entrance of the Scheldt. That same month, the Allied commanders ordered the First Canadian Army to retake control of the seventy-mile river which runs almost entirely through the Netherlands. The subsequent battle became known as the Battle of the Scheldt and lasted from October 2nd to November 8th, 1944.

Operation Switchback

In the summer of 1944, Gustave was fighting with the Canadian army in Northern Africa when he heard the news that officers of Belgian descent were being asked to help liberate Belgium. He immediately signed up, excited to contribute to the liberation of Belgium. By the end October, he joined the Canadian army in Belgium. At that time, the Canadian army had already liberated most of the Scheldt except for the all-important entrance of the Scheldt, which remained in the hands of the Nazis. This prompted the

Canadian army to launch Operation Switchback, with the sole purpose of reclaiming this crucial area from the Nazis. So close to Knokke, Gustave could hardly wait for Operation Switchback to get off the ground. Everybody knew that this would to be a deadly battle. The Nazis were determined to fight to the last man to block the Allies from accessing the Scheldt. On top of that, it would be next to impossible to advance with tanks and other heavy equipment as the Nazis had flooded the entire area, turning the land into a huge mud field.

The encircled area indicates the only remaining stronghold that was held by the Nazis after the rest of the river had already been liberated.

Gustave, because of his intimate knowledge of the area, was put in charge of liberating Knokke. On the night of

October 31st, 1944, he was put in charge of leading a vanguard of thirty Canadian soldiers into the center of Knokke. They would be followed by a larger contingent of infantry. They were within a few hundred yards from city hall, when pockets of Nazi soldiers challenged them, putting up a fierce defense. After a while, more and more Nazis were no longer determined to fight to the last man. They surrendered and were taken prisoner by the infantry.

Gustave knew that the German Commander had his headquarters at city hall. Once the commander realized that he was completely surrounded, he reluctantly raised the white flag. Two high-level Canadian delegates, one speaking English, the other French, were brought in for the formal signing. They asked Gustave to join them in the meeting as a translator. He would need to listen to anything that was said in German and translate it into English or French. Of course, he was also fluent in the local Flemish dialect. The meeting didn't exactly take place as planned. To everyone's astonishment, the German commander continued to act as if he was still in charge. This prompted one of the Canadian delegates to abruptly rebuke him to stop acting like he was in control. He'd better started following instead of giving orders.

Once Gustave's presence was no longer needed, he went to check on the other prisoners. A shock shot up his spine when he saw two prisoners hiding in a corner. They were wearing the black uniform of the dreaded Gestapo! Without hesitation, he walked up to them and stripped them of their badges. What a sweet revenge after all that he and Louis had gone through. Finally, he rushed home to embrace his wife whom he hadn't seen in four years. The reunion was very emotional. Word about the liberation of Knokke and Gustave's role had already spread like wildfire. Hundreds of people had assembled in front of his house. When Gustave appeared on the balcony to wave at them, a loud hooray erupted, welcoming him home.

What about Louis? After the war was over, he went back to Belgium. Although he enjoyed his time with the navy and the respect he received from leadership, he was glad that it was over. He was looking forward to no longer having to blindly obey military orders. Once again, he could be his own boss! With the money saved during his time with the Navy, he bought himself a seaworthy fishing boat and replaced the existing engine with the newest model available. On his first trip out, he could not have been happier.

Historic Epilogue

Although Knokke was liberated on November 2nd, it took another week before both sides of the Scheldt were freed from the Nazis. At the end of the five-week offensive, the victorious First Canadian Army had taken 41,043 Nazis prisoners. The Allies suffered 12,873 casualties (killed, wounded, or missing), 6,367 of them being Canadian. 848 Canadian soldiers are buried nearby in a Canadian War cemetery.

The end of the Battle of the Scheldt didn't automatically mean that it was safe for ships to sail to Antwerp. The Nazis had blanketed the river with sea mines. It took mine sweepers another month, until November 28th, 1944 before the first military supply safely boat made it to Antwerp.

Still, there was more to come. Hitler, realizing that the Allied Forces were focused on opening the Scheldt, decided to take advantage of the situation. On December 16th, 1944, against all expectations, he launched an all-out counter-offensive in the Belgian Ardennes, which became known as the Battle of the Bulge. His goal was not to reconquer Europe but to split the enemy in two and force them to negotiate a peace treaty. It was a terrible battle. America suffered 75,000 casualties and the Nazis 80,000 to 100,000. The battle ended on January 25th, 1945, and two weeks later, on February 4th, 1945, Belgium was finally fully liberated. On May 9th, 1945, Germany surrendered unconditionally. World War II officially ended after Japan surrendered on September 2nd, 1945.

About the Co-Authors

Luc De Brouckere grew up in a small town along the North Sea in Belgium. He is an electronics engineer with a Ph.D. in Solid State Physics. He worked in the United States, Belgium, the Netherlands, England, and Switzerland. Thirty years ago, he moved with his family to the USA and settled in the Boston area. He has since retired. He recently wrote a 410-pages book entitled "Cultural Heritage of an Enfant Terrible". It is a private luxury edition limited to close family and friends. He is an avid sailor and loves soccer.

Niels De Brouckere was born in Naperville, Illinois to a Belgian father and American mother. He is a full-time high school student enrolled in AP European History. His primary interests include spending time with friends, playing soccer and eating Belgian food. This is Niels' first publication outside of school.

Ian De Brouckere was born in Naperville, Illinois to a Belgian father and American mother. He is a full-time high school student with varied interests in math, chorus, soccer, and his dogs. Writing this book helped him round out his appreciation for his Belgian heritage which had been mostly limited to Belgian food and sports.

Made in United States
North Haven, CT
04 August 2022

22296984R00075